Samuel French Acting Edition

I0591773

Red-Handed Otter

by Ethan Lipton

SAMUELFRENCH.COM   SAMUELFRENCH.CO.UK

FOR PRODUCTION ENQUIRIES

UNITED STATES AND CANADA
Info@SamuelFrench.com
1-866-598-8449

UNITED KINGDOM AND EUROPE
Plays@SamuelFrench.co.uk
020-7255-4302

Each title is subject to availability from Samuel French, depending upon country of performance. Please be aware that *RED-HANDED OTTER* may not be licensed by Samuel French in your territory. Professional and amateur producers should contact the nearest Samuel French office or licensing partner to verify availability.

MUSIC USE NOTE

Licensees are solely responsible for obtaining formal written permission from copyright owners to use copyrighted music in the performance of this play and are strongly cautioned to do so. If no such permission is obtained by the licensee, then the licensee must use only original music that the licensee owns and controls. Licensees are solely responsible and liable for all music clearances and shall indemnify the copyright owners of the play(s) and their licensing agent, Samuel French, against any costs, expenses, losses and liabilities arising from the use of music by licensees. Please contact the appropriate music licensing authority in your territory for the rights to any incidental music.

IMPORTANT BILLING AND CREDIT REQUIREMENTS

If you have obtained performance rights to this title, please refer to your licensing agreement for important billing and credit requirements.

RED-HANDED OTTER was first produced by the Playwrights Realm (Katherine Kovner, Founding Artistic Director; Renee Blinkwolt, Producing Director) on September 12, 2012. The performance was directed by Mike Donohue, with sets by Andrew Boyce, costumes by Moria Sine Clinton, lighting by Lucrecia Briceño, sound by Jill BC Du Boff, props by Andrew Diaz, and video by Daniel Vatsky. The production stage manager was Joanne E. McInerney. The cast was as follows:

DONALD	Bobby Moreno
PAUL	Matthew Maher
ESTELLE	Quincy Tyler Bernstine
ANGELA	Rebecca Henderson
RANDY	Gibson Frazier

CHARACTERS

DONALD – late twenties
PAUL – early forties
ESTELLE – early forties
ANGELA – early thirties
RANDY – mid-forties

SETTING

The security guards' post in a big, cold building.

AUTHOR'S NOTES

There is a lot of listening in this play. Listening to music. Being in silence. Long stretches where nothing happens. These moments of silence are essential to our understanding of these characters. Their workplace is a world of non-events. This doesn't mean scenes should ever lack urgency, only that we need to feel how little typically happens in their lives to feel the impact of what happens in the course of the play.

Scene One

(The security guards' post. A long desk and chairs for two. Off to the side, a row of lockers.)

(A banquette of TV monitors hang on the back wall, showing security camera shots of building life – the more TVs the better – though there is very little of it to show. The room on the whole is shallow and flat.)

*(**DONALD** is mid-shift. **PAUL** is almost finished with his shift and will pack over the course of the scene. For now, they are both still, listening to a piece of Polish contemporary classical music* on the office boombox. It is one of the saddest pieces of music ever, and they are listening with purpose. **PAUL** is heartsick, on the verge of exploding, yet he is keeping this fact from **DONALD**.)*

(It's 3:45 a.m. on Monday.)

DONALD. What *is* this?

PAUL. *(After a moment.)* Third Symphony. Robin Wallace soprano.

DONALD. *(Listens.)* That's some heavy business.

PAUL. It's hell on earth, man.

DONALD. *(Listens.)* Sounds like somebody being dragged out to sea.

PAUL. It's a mother, mourning her child.

---

*A license to produce *Red-Handed Otter* does not include a performance license for any third-party or copyrighted music. Licensees should create an original composition or use music in the public domain. "Third Symphony" by Robin Wallace is a fictional title. For further information, please see Music Use Note on page 3.

DONALD. Can I borrow it?

PAUL. You can have it. But be careful. Robin Wallace will stab you in the fucking heart.

DONALD. *(Listens.)* Have you ever heard of Donna Summer?

PAUL. *(Considers, no judgement.)* Yes, I have heard of Donna Summer.

DONALD. You own any?

PAUL. *(Considers.)* No.

DONALD. You got anything against her?

PAUL. *(Considers.)* Not that I know of.

DONALD. *(Listens.)* Paul, I want to bring you some Donna Summer.

PAUL. All right.

DONALD. *Bad Girls*.

PAUL. That's an album?

DONALD. Yeah, although she had a ton of hits. You've probably just heard a single or two, right?

PAUL. Possibly.

DONALD. Well then, we'll set you up with *Bad Girls*, see how you do with that. Then we can talk about *The Wanderer*. Damn, this is exciting. Finally getting to give back, after all the great music you've given me. It's exciting.

> *(They listen.* **PAUL** *begins to weep.)*

You okay?

PAUL. Jennifer died.

DONALD. No. Paul. When?

PAUL. Saturday.

DONALD. What happened?

PAUL. I walk in the door after my shift, five a.m., she's great. I make us something to eat, read the paper. She takes a nap, in the hat. I have this floppy hat that I keep on the table.

DONALD. Right?

PAUL. I go off to bed, watch a little TV. She crawls in next to me, works her way under the covers. When I wake up that afternoon, she's right there under my arm, but she isn't sleeping.

DONALD. She wasn't moving at all?

PAUL. I've had moments like that, before? Where she's so still you're like, what the fuck, is she breathing? And then you touch her and all of a sudden she'll reach her paw out ten feet across the room, and you know she's okay. But...nope.

DONALD. Fuck, man.

PAUL. What can you do, right? What can you do?

DONALD. *(A moment.)* How old was she?

PAUL. Seventeen.

DONALD. Seventeen years old?! And you had her forever, right?

PAUL. Found her in a garbage can behind my old apartment.

DONALD. In a garbage can. I mean, what was she doing in there?

PAUL. Just chillin'.

DONALD. Jesus.

PAUL. Just relaxing.

DONALD. And from there she goes on to be seventeen years old?

PAUL. Yeah.

DONALD. I mean that is something. That's a good life.

PAUL. And it wasn't always easy for her.

DONALD. How could it be?

PAUL. She had her dark days. But then...

> *(Wailing grief.)*

AAWHWHWHWHWHWH! AAWHWHWHWWH WHHW!

> *(After a moment.)*

Sorry.

(Punishing himself.)

PAUL. Fucking idiot. Stupid fucking idiot.

DONALD. Hey. Not stupid. That was a big relationship, for like a lot of years.

PAUL. She totally brought joy to my life.

DONALD. Yeah she did.

PAUL. I was such a bitter asshole before I met her, you know? I used to tear people's heads off just for fun.

DONALD. She changed your life.

PAUL. Those fucked up teeth? And the bald spots on her head? You'd get up out of bed, and she'd guard you like she was playing man-to-man defense, sidestepping to stay in front of you all the way to the bathroom.

DONALD. She was a superstar.

PAUL. What else could you call her?

DONALD. That cat was a Hall of Fame cat.

PAUL. She was a fucking Hall of Famer, Don. Maybe one of the top five cats ever.

DONALD. I don't think that's out of line.

PAUL. And I know, okay? Everyone thinks their cat is the best cat, and they should –

DONALD. Of course –

PAUL. But they're wrong. You know? I mean, yes, I'm sure your cat is a great cat, guy, and by all means, love the fuck out of each other, but let's not be silly about it, okay? I've had other cats. As a kid we had cats, they were great cats, but compared to Jennifer? If you just look at it objectively?

DONALD. Top five all-time.

PAUL. We're talking about one of the best cats in history!

(Considers.)

You met her?

DONALD. No, but I feel like I did. I mean, I heard.

PAUL. From Angela?

DONALD. Angela, from you...

PAUL. She talked about her?

DONALD. Everybody talked about her, man. She was one of the characters in our lives, she got her own conversations and speculations...

PAUL. What kind of speculations?

DONALD. Like, I don't know – no, okay, tell me this: What was she thinking, Paul, when she would sleep all day with the covers up to her neck and her head on the pillow, like some kinda little animated doll?

PAUL. You heard about that?

DONALD. Yes!

PAUL. What kind of supernatural cat does that!?

DONALD. I don't know!

PAUL. She was like a pretend cat, she had so much personality.

DONALD. And didn't she get her nail caught in the screen one time?

PAUL. Oh my God! By the time I got home she wasn't even fighting it. She was just sitting on the window sill, her paw sticking up in the air like she was hailing a cab.

DONALD. See, I know about that and I didn't even hear about it from you, that's what I'm saying.

PAUL. Angela told you?

DONALD. I don't know, I mean it might have been Angela, or Estelle, Randy, Henry –

PAUL. Henry never met Jennifer –

DONALD. Okay –

PAUL. I would never let Henry near Jennifer –

DONALD. So not Henry, it wasn't Henry, but somebody told me. I mean, she was one of the gang, Paul. She was one of us.

PAUL. I never thought I'd be in this place without her. Fifteen years. Fifteen years ago – this was before Henry, before Randy even – I sat in that chair –

(**DONALD**'s *chair.*)

PAUL. – Telling Arnie Concepcion, "Six months. I'm gonna be here six months. Just paying some bills before I go back to school." Arnie Concepcion. Lives upstate with his sister now, goes fishing whenever he wants; last I heard he was working his way through Tolstoy. And I'm still here. Still getting off work at four in the morning, going home to the same shitty apartment. Except now, I don't even have a cat.

> (**PAUL** *stands. He takes the CD out of the boombox and offers it to* **DONALD**, *who takes it.*)
>
> (**PAUL** *goes to his locker.*)

DONALD. See you Wednesday?

PAUL. (*Muttering; not quite audible.*) I don't fucking care anymore.

DONALD. Sorry?

> (**PAUL** *pulls a backpack out of his locker. He opens the pack, inspects it. He returns to* **DONALD**, *offering him a baseball cap and a graphic novel, which he eyes with disgust.*)

PAUL. Take care of yourself, Don. Angela too. She's a good person.

> (**PAUL** *starts to exit.*)

DONALD. I lost my best friend once. Still think about him every day.

PAUL. (*Stopping in spite of himself.*) What was his name?

DONALD. Dan.

PAUL. Dan? Don and Dan.

DONALD. Yeah, we were quite a pair.

PAUL. (*Considers.*) What happened to him?

DONALD. He swam away. He was an otter. A red-handed otter. They're rare but not as rare as you might think. He'd been abandoned as a pup, so I nursed him back to health, first with kitty formula that I stole from the pharmacy, and later with crawfish I caught in the river behind our house. That's where I found him, under this big rock where I used to hide out from my stepdad. My mom was stationed in Germany and my stepdad, he was sort of a drunk, used to… Anyway, one day I'm out by the river, and I hear this little whimper, right? So I look under the rock, and there's Dan. And as soon he sees me, his eyes get real big, and I just start laughing. I'm like, "Dude, what are you doing?"

(After a moment.)

I kept him in a shoe box that I stashed under my bed, like for the first two weeks, and then when he got too smelly I moved him out to the boathouse next door. We had this neighbor, Mrs. Alstadt, big house, could've fit our place in there five or six different ways, but she lived alone, and nobody used the boathouse except her grandkids in the summer, and so I put Dan in there, let him have free rein of the life vests and canoes.

PAUL. How'd he get away?

DONALD. Well, yeah. See, I knew I couldn't keep him. Guy wouldn't stop growing. And Joshua, my stepdad, I mean if he ever found him that've been the end for both of us, so, I made a plan. One day Joshua took off to sell wood – every few weeks he'd sell firewood out of his truck, make himself feel like he was contributing – and first thing I did was bring Dan inside the house and make him a special goodbye breakfast.

PAUL. Uh-huh. And what was that?

DONALD. Sardines and toast.

PAUL. All right.

DONALD. And then I gave him a bath.

PAUL. Wait a second, you gave him a bath?

DONALD. Yeah, well, he hadn't been in water since I found him, so I didn't even know if he could swim.

PAUL. Could he?

DONALD. Oh man, he zipped around that tub like a demon. After I dried him off, and brought him out to the living room. We had this wobbly old table, this old Sally Ann coffee table – my mom let me pick it out when we first moved in – and I put a towel down on it, got Dan up there, and then I gave him a one-hour, professional-style massage.

PAUL. Timeout. You gave him a what?

DONALD. A massage.

PAUL. What do you mean?

DONALD. Okay, see, there was this lady down the road who used to give massages out of her house.

PAUL. Uh-huh?

DONALD. Legitimate ones.

PAUL. All right.

DONALD. And sometimes on my way home from school I might watch her through a window.

PAUL. Giving massages to strangers.

DONALD. Yeah, exactly. And these people, Paul, I'm telling you: they went into that house looking like crumpled up trolls, and they walked out looking like royalty. Like they'd been hauling around a two-ton brick their whole lives, and that massage lady and her giant ponytail had just smashed it to pieces. I remember asking myself, one day when I was watching, does anybody ever do this for animals? 'Cause I think that's the kinda shit they could really get into. And I asked my teacher, Mrs. Rybin, and she said no, to the best of her knowledge nobody else in town was offering that service. So I said okay then, that's what I'm going to do. When I grow up, I'm going to start a business that gives professional massages to animals.

PAUL. Animals get massaged all the time, Don.

DONALD. Do they?

PAUL. That's why we call them pets. Because we pet them.

DONALD. I'm not talking about a pat on the butt, okay? I'm talking about getting in there, so their muscles are seriously being kneaded and stimulated, working out all the trauma.

PAUL. What makes you think an animal needs that?

DONALD. Well, I don't know about you, man, but I've known some pretty stressed-out animals. Look, I'm not trying to get you to invest in my pet massage company –

PAUL. No-no-no, I know –

DONALD. There is no company, it's just a dream I had as a kid.

PAUL. Does it work?

DONALD. I mean, it's hard to say as a business model, but –

PAUL. Did it work on Dan?

DONALD. Oh, yeah. Yeah, he lay there still as he could, and he let me just wring it all out for him. Now, was it professional grade? I doubt it. I was nine years old. Plus it was the first one I ever gave, so it's probably a miracle I didn't break his neck. But was he a more open, more relaxed otter when I finished?

PAUL. He was.

DONALD. He took a two-hour nap on the table. I cleaned the whole house, vacuumed, everything, he didn't move. Later, after he woke up, I brought him out to the river. Set him down in the dirt. He walked over to the water and...slipped right in. Swam off with the current. I hopped up onto the rock, you know, so I could watch him, and right before he dipped behind the trees, he rolled over onto his side and waved goodbye. Stuck his little red paw in the air and... I don't know. I told myself it was a wave.

PAUL. And he never came back?

DONALD. At first I couldn't forgive myself, for letting him go. But in the end I figured, the reason he never came back was: our relationship was complete. And we didn't have to be together in order to be "together." We just were – are – together. And what we have, it's not like a picture on a shelf or a special jacket I put on once a year to feel all warm and fuzzy. It's under my skin. He changed me. That's the part that reminded me of you and Jennifer.

PAUL. She used to sit on my head.

DONALD. She still does.

Scene Two

*(At work, in a utility closet. **ANGELA**, a guard, is seated on **DONALD**'s lap. **DONALD** is off duty. They are making out. It's 3:06 p.m. on Tuesday.)*

DONALD. Do we make him something to eat?

ANGELA. I could make him some soup.

DONALD. Yeah?

ANGELA. Some tomato soup?

DONALD. God, I love your tomato soup.

ANGELA. Yeah, so does he. After we broke up, when he was leaving me those notes in my locker, one of them was all about my tomato soup.

DONALD. Right. That might be awkward then.

ANGELA. Might be.

(They make out.)

DONALD. What about mac and cheese? Like if I made him a big casserole dish of my famous mac and cheese?

ANGELA. *(Why not?)* Yeah.

DONALD. I just think we have to do something.

ANGELA. Make him some mac and cheese.

DONALD. Did you leave him a message?

ANGELA. Uh-huh.

DONALD. What'd you say?

ANGELA. I said, "I'm sorry for your loss."

DONALD. That's nice.

ANGELA. Yeah? That seems okay?

DONALD. That's great.

ANGELA. Yeah, I was just like, "She was a super cat, Paul, and I know how much you cared about her, and I'm sorry for your loss."

DONALD. Perfect. So perfect.

(They make out.)

DONALD. Do we know if he even likes mac and cheese?

ANGELA. Baby, I think he's going to be okay. You know? In the big picture? Like, if I had to pick one thing Paul knows how to manage incredibly well, I'd pick depression. I mean, rage or hygiene? Maybe not. But depression? For Paul? That's like mustard to a hot dog.

> (*Lights up on the guard post, where* **RANDY**, *on duty, speaks on a walkie-talkie, a newspaper by his side.*)

RANDY. Two, this is One. Come in, Two.

DONALD. He just sounded so defeated, you know? Almost...

ANGELA. What?

DONALD. I don't know, like he was saying goodbye.

RANDY. Two, this is One, are you still in the toilette?

> (**ANGELA** *answers her walkie.*)

ANGELA. Yes Randy, I'm still in the bathroom.

RANDY. Yeah?

ANGELA. Yes.

RANDY. Whatcha doing in there?

ANGELA. I'm busy, being in the bathroom.

RANDY. That's cool.

ANGELA. What do you need, Randy?

RANDY. I was just wondering. If you. Want to order something to eat.

ANGELA. No thank you.

RANDY. I'm leaning toward Little India.

ANGELA. Great.

RANDY. In which case I could do the lunch special solo, or we could coordinate.

ANGELA. I'm really not that hungry –

RANDY. Or I could order from Chicken Man. You like Chicken Man, don't you?

ANGELA. No, as a matter of fact, I don't like Chicken Man. I don't trust his chickens.

RANDY. You think Chicken Man's using funny chickens?

ANGELA. Randy, I'm not hungry.

RANDY. All right. Anything for you, Don?

DONALD. No thanks –

(*Realizing he's caught.*)

RANDY. Bah!

ANGELA. Thanks for minding your own business.

RANDY. You know, off-duty employees are not supposed to be loitering on the premises –

(**ANGELA** *turns off her walkie-talkie.*)

ANGELA. You were saying? About Paul?

DONALD. Oh, yeah. I don't know.

ANGELA. But like, he was saying goodbye, like he was going to quit?

DONALD. Not necessarily that.

ANGELA. (*Considers.*) Do we need to call the police?

DONALD. The police?

ANGELA. Because we can call them and have someone go over there.

DONALD. No, no, that would be way too much.

ANGELA. I mean, not if he's in a bad way.

(*After a moment.*)

What do you want to do?

DONALD. Maybe we should go over there.

ANGELA. You and me?

DONALD. Yeah.

ANGELA. Together?

DONALD. Yeah! And then on top of that, we bring him some of my delicious mac and cheese!

ANGELA. (*A breath.*) Okay.

DONALD. Or we could bring him something else.

ANGELA. Yeah. Something that isn't so cheesy.

DONALD. You don't like my mac and cheese?

ANGELA. I like it a lot. It's just, well, it's very cheesy.

DONALD. Right?

ANGELA. And I imagine he's doing a lot of drinking these days.

DONALD. Right.

ANGELA. Could be sort of an unpleasant situation.

DONALD. Right. We could get him a cat.

ANGELA. Yeah, that'd be funny.

DONALD. Come on!

ANGELA. We're not getting him a cat.

DONALD. Why not? Come on, let's get him a cat!

ANGELA. Don, Jennifer was the love of his life.

DONALD. Exactly.

ANGELA. And so, what, now that she's gone, you want to...?

DONALD. Help him get back in the game.

ANGELA. By getting him a brand-new cat?

DONALD. No, silly. We'd get him a rescue.

ANGELA. Baby, you can't just get back in the game after the last one ends. It isn't a tournament.

DONALD. Well, what about us?

ANGELA. What about us?

DONALD. I'm just saying...

ANGELA. You think this is me getting back in the game?

DONALD. No –

ANGELA. You think it's too soon, is that what you're saying?

DONALD. No, the opposite, the opposite. I'm saying maybe, if your heart is already open, that's the perfect time to let someone else in. Because you're soft, you're ready. Whereas if you wait until you're totally over it, then your heart could get cold and impenetrable.

ANGELA. *(Off his huge smile.)* Stop.

DONALD. I can't.

ANGELA. Don, do you trust me?

    (He just looks at her.)

It's not a rhetorical question.

DONALD. Yes, yes, sorry.

ANGELA. Okay, then. Even if it doesn't make sense to you now, I want you to try to hear me, and trust me when I say: We don't want to get Paul a cat. As much as we want him to feel better, that's just not the way to do it.

DONALD. *(Sitting back, appraising.)* But if I can't give him mac and cheese and I can't get him a cat –

ANGELA. I'm going to drop off a card. And you are going to figure out what's right for you to do.

(She kisses him. They make out.)

Scene Three

(In the guards' post **ESTELLE** *knits a scarf while speaking on the open channel of her walkie-talkie to* **RANDY**, *who is patrolling a different floor – we don't see him.)*

(It's 10:32 a.m. on Wednesday.)

RANDY. Now, at that point I'd only had a guinea pig and a hermit crab.

ESTELLE. What about dogs?

RANDY. Well, dogs, we always had dogs, but as far as what I was personally in charge of.

ESTELLE. Uh-huh?

RANDY. What was that guinea pig's name?

ESTELLE. *(To herself, re: the sweater.)* Please tell me I didn't just do that.

RANDY. Huh. I can't remember. Billy? Bugsy?

ESTELLE. Oh well.

RANDY. Was it Bugsy?

ESTELLE. What was the hermit crab called?

RANDY. Oscar.

ESTELLE. And what did you get a hermit crab for?

RANDY. Because I wanted one. Didn't you?

ESTELLE. I didn't even know what a hermit crab was until maybe high school.

RANDY. But didn't you want one as soon as you found out?

ESTELLE. Not really.

RANDY. See, as soon as I found out what a hermit crab was, that's what I had to have.

ESTELLE. Why?

RANDY. It's the perfect combination of a wet and dry pet.

ESTELLE. I see. Did you and Oscar get along well?

RANDY. Oh yeah. Sometimes he was walking, sometimes he was hiding: You didn't know what he'd do next. I'd put him down on the carpet, let him go off on his little journeys, pretend he was crossing a mountain range.

ESTELLE. He was up for anything, huh?

RANDY. Yeah. Just so long as you didn't rush him.

ESTELLE. Why would you rush a hermit crab?

RANDY. Well, he was slow.

ESTELLE. Isn't that the idea?

RANDY. Yes, but…sometimes you got the feeling it might be on purpose.

ESTELLE. How do you mean?

RANDY. Like he was capable of going faster, he just didn't feel like it.

ESTELLE. Uh-huh?

RANDY. So now and then I might give him a nudge. For encouragement.

ESTELLE. Okay.

RANDY. Hey, even I need a kick in the ass now and then.

ESTELLE. You like to be flicked across the room, is that right?

RANDY. Whoa, whoa, whoa. Who said anything about being flicked?

ESTELLE. You did.

RANDY. No, I said nudge. I would nudge him –

ESTELLE. Yeah, but I think you meant flick, you would flick him –

RANDY. I never did anything more than a scoot, and it was always with the best of intentions.

ESTELLE. Well, I'm glad we're having this conversation. Here I'd been thinking you were such an upstanding gentleman, always doing what's right. Come to find out, you're nothing but a little ol' hermit crab flicker.

RANDY. I stopped nudging Oscar as soon as I found out he didn't like it! I happen to be very good with animals.

ESTELLE. I didn't mean anything.

RANDY. I don't care what you think of me, Estelle.

*(There's a rustling sound on **RANDY**'s floor.
ESTELLE puts down her knitting.)*

ESTELLE. I'm sure you took excellent care of him.

RANDY. *(After a moment.)* It took me a while...to realize I was supposed to be cleaning his tank.

ESTELLE. Well, that's not a crime. How long did it take?

RANDY. About six months.

ESTELLE. Hold on.

RANDY. I didn't know –

ESTELLE. You didn't clean his tank for –

RANDY. I didn't have all the facts, okay? I thought if something was wet, that meant it was also clean.

ESTELLE. Uh-huh?

RANDY. I figured, if Oscar comes from the ocean, and the ocean is wet, then Oscar must be naturally clean. When are they going to fix the lights up in here? It's a god damn fire hazard.

ESTELLE. You didn't know hermit crabs went to the bathroom?

RANDY. It never occurred to me.

ESTELLE. Didn't it smell?

RANDY. I don't know, Estelle, sure, it smelled like my room. Like me and Oscar living our lives.

*(A bigger rustle on **RANDY**'s floor.)*

ESTELLE. What was that? Randy? What was that sound?

RANDY. I did the best I could with that hermit crab.

(Another rustle.)

ESTELLE. Sixteen North, right? I'm pulling it up.

*(On the control panel **ESTELLE** calls up a camera shot of **RANDY**'s floor, where we see him patrolling, dimly lit with his flashlight.)*

RANDY. Jennifer adored me, ugly-ass mongrel cat; cat eczema flaking all over your lap.

*(**RANDY** turns off his flashlight.)*

ESTELLE. Hey, turn your light back on.

RANDY. My eyes work better in the dark.

ESTELLE. *(After a moment.)* Randy?

RANDY. Anyway.

> (**RANDY** *patrols the space in the darkness, out of view of the camera.)*

ESTELLE. *(Trying to make up.)* I once had a smoke detector with a bad battery in it? And it would go off like every thirty seconds. I didn't change the battery in it for over a year.

RANDY. *(Despite himself.)* So the thing would flash all the time?

ESTELLE. Not flash. Beep.

RANDY. Every thirty seconds?

ESTELLE. For over a year.

RANDY. What about when you were sleeping?

ESTELLE. Every thirty seconds.

RANDY. Didn't it wake you up?

ESTELLE. At first, yeah, but after a few days, I didn't even notice. Probably folded it right into my dreams.

RANDY. Was it loud?

ESTELLE. Yeah.

RANDY. How loud?

ESTELLE. BEEP!

RANDY. Damn! Every time?

ESTELLE. BEEP!

RANDY. Okay, you're going to puncture my ear.

ESTELLE. Every now and then someone would walk into my room and be like, what is that? And I'd hear it again, as if for the first time, and be like, dang, I gotta change that battery.

RANDY. So why not do it?

ESTELLE. Why not exactly? Why not see what's right there in front of us?

RANDY. *(After a moment.)* Did you change the battery or not?

ESTELLE. Is that what you think I'm talking about?

RANDY. I don't know what you're talking about.

ESTELLE. I'm talking about changing your life.

RANDY. When you can't even change a battery?

ESTELLE. I did change the battery!

RANDY. Okay!

(*After a moment, gently.*)

How'd you do it?

ESTELLE. One day I was like, "Hey, you know what? I'm going to change that battery for real." And I climbed up onto my dresser – no. First I had to find a new battery. I went into the kitchen and I opened the drawer where we kept the new batteries, and I got a new battery. *Then* I went to my room, and I got up on the dresser, and I took off the cover, and I took out the old battery, and I put in the new one. And after that, it didn't make a peep. And for the rest of that whole day, I was like, "Hell yeah. I can do anything."

(**RANDY** *comes into view on the monitor again.*)

RANDY. *(Considers.)* I had a feeling the tank should be cleaned. I had a feeling. I just didn't know how it was supposed to happen.

ESTELLE. Makes sense.

RANDY. My mom came into my room, she practically passed out from the fumes, she thought it was a gas leak. But once she pointed it out to me, I did clean the tank, and I did so regularly from then on.

ESTELLE. How long did you have him for? Randy? How long did you have Oscar?

RANDY. He got eaten by my dog.

ESTELLE. No.

RANDY. I was out of the room, chasing my brother – he was always stealing my shit – I leave Oscar on the carpet for one minute, and when I come back our dog Dandy is sitting there, looking me right in the eye, chomping away on Oscar as if he were so many corn nuts. And nobody threw a party for me, I'll tell you that much. Nobody even likes Paul. Why throw a party for someone nobody likes?

ESTELLE. I like Paul.

RANDY. But is that how you want to spend your Friday night, showing up here so you can waste your time trying to cheer him up?

ESTELLE. What would we do instead?

> (**ESTELLE** *stands, aghast at the realization that she has just asked him out.*)

RANDY.	ESTELLE.
Huh?	What?

RANDY. What'd you say?

> (**ESTELLE** *turns off the camera on 16 North.*)

ESTELLE. Dandy's the one who got hit by a car?

RANDY. That's not what you said.

ESTELLE. Yes it is.

> (*After an awkward silence.*)

Dandy's the one who got hit by a car?

RANDY. No, that was Molly.

ESTELLE. Oh yeah. But that wasn't your fault.

RANDY. Listen, I closed the gate, she pushed it back open. Hound dogs are extremely stubborn, and Molly was as stubborn as they come. She ate a wallet. A sponge. A stick of butter. A pair of glasses. Set of laminated placemats.

Scene Four

(In the guards' post **PAUL** *is on the late shift, seated at the desk.)*

*(***DONALD**, **ANGELA**, **ESTELLE**, *and* **RANDY** *are gathered around in civvies. There is a case of beer, a six-pack of wine coolers, an open packet of store-bought cookies, and much of this has already been consumed.* **ESTELLE** *and* **PAUL** *are drinking the most. Special disco music* plays on the boombox, and* **DONALD** *has it in his bones – he can't stop moving to the beat.* **DONALD** *is playing host, opening beers for people and generally keeping the party going.)*

(It's 1:27 a.m. on Saturday.)

ESTELLE. So you got another rabbit to keep the first one company.

ANGELA. No.

PAUL. Her parents wouldn't let her.

ANGELA. I took her to school to get her mated.

ESTELLE. You did what?

ANGELA. I took her to school, to mate her with another rabbit.

PAUL. Because Cinnamon was lonely.

ESTELLE. But if you knew your parents wouldn't let you have a second rabbit –

ANGELA. It wasn't a totally thought-through plan. I was eleven.

RANDY. Old enough to be pimping out rabbits.

ANGELA. I wasn't pimping her out. I just wanted her to have a little –

RANDY. Pimping.

ANGELA. Social interaction.

(*They listen to the music.*)

ESTELLE. Why take her to school, though?

ANGELA. We had this really great animal husbandry program, like a fenced-in area, where you could practice taking care of them, all these goats and chickens and rabbits –

ESTELLE. You had one of those at your school?

ANGELA. Yeah.

RANDY. And you were encouraged to mate these animals with animals you brought from home.

ANGELA. All right, you know what? Forget it.

RANDY. What?

ANGELA. It's not that big a deal, I don't even know why I'm telling the story –

PAUL. Because I want to hear it.

DONALD. We all want to hear it.

ESTELLE. Yeah.

PAUL. Which is why Randy is going to shut his fucking mouth.

RANDY. Oh, is that what I'm going to do?

ESTELLE. Did your parents know you were taking the rabbit to school?

ANGELA. No.

ESTELLE. How did you get it there?

ANGELA. Well –

PAUL. She snuck it into her backpack and took it on the bus.

ESTELLE. You smuggled the rabbit to school on the bus?

PAUL. Isn't that awesome?

ANGELA. My house was like fifteen miles away.

ESTELLE. And what'd you do once you got her to school?

ANGELA. I took her to the animal husbandry area, and then I put her in a cage with this other really nice, handsome rabbit, who was white with gray spots.

RANDY. What color was Cinnamon?

ANGELA & PAUL. Cinnamon colored.

RANDY. Okay, okay –

PAUL. That's why she named her Cinnamon –

RANDY. I understand that now.

    (They listen.)

ESTELLE. Where were the teachers when all this was going on?

RANDY. Good question.

ANGELA. Well, there was just the animal husbandry lady, but there were always lots of kids coming and going, and it was right next to the parking lot, where all the older kids would be smoking, so it was pretty chaotic.

ESTELLE. What kind of a school was this?

ANGELA. A magnet school. I was supposed to be a doctor.

RANDY. So you drop her off with the white-and-gray rabbit –

ANGELA. Right, and then I go to class. And at the end of the day I pick her up and take her home.

DONALD. Did you visit her during the day?

ANGELA. I think so.

ESTELLE. And then what, after you get her home?

ANGELA. Nothing. She didn't look any different, didn't act any different. A few weeks later I'm holding her on my lap and I decide to give her a more thorough inspection.

ESTELLE. Right?

ANGELA. And wouldn't you know it, as I'm checking her underside –

RANDY. She's a boy –

ANGELA. I see what looks like a little rabbit pecker.

RANDY. Called it!

ANGELA. Actually, I couldn't tell for sure. And it wasn't just me, I found out later, with rabbits it's hard to figure out.

ESTELLE. I don't know where this story is going now.

ANGELA. At that point I start checking her parts like every time I pick her up. One day I think she's a boy, the next I think she's a girl. One afternoon I go to say hi to her after school and I see that she's pulling out these big chunks of hair from her chest and hopping around like a crazy rabbit. And I go tell my dad, because I think something's wrong, and he says, "She's nesting." I'm like, "What's that mean?" And he goes, "It means she's going to have babies."

ESTELLE. So she is a girl!

ANGELA. Yes. And I'm like, fuck, nesting? And my dad's like, "Angela? Why is Cinnamon going to have babies?" And I'm like, "I took her to school for Show and Tell, maybe something happened to her there?"

RANDY. And how did he like that answer?

ANGELA. You know what? I have to say, that was sort of a magic wand day for my dad. He made her this box out of wood, so she could collect all her fur, and then he built her a hutch that was like twice as big as the one she already had, and he put it out by the side of the house. And he hung a work light over the hutch from this big old lemon tree that we had. I remember, my parents had friends over that night, which I always liked, but after dinner I went straight back to my room and I sat by the window, and I watched her all night, giving birth, like, over and over.

ESTELLE. Wow.

ANGELA. In the morning we went out to look, and you couldn't touch, but you could see them. It looked like they were stuck together.

ESTELLE. How many?

ANGELA. Ten.

ESTELLE. Wow.

RANDY. Were they alive?

ANGELA. All but one, which my dad said was really good for a first litter.

PAUL. It's amazing.

ESTELLE. And what in the world did you do with them all?

ANGELA. The first couple of weeks it was pretty exciting. Just checking up on them, making sure they were okay, watching them eat. Then at about three weeks you could hold them.

ESTELLE. Were they soft?

ANGELA. Estelle, they were literally the softest things I've ever touched.

RANDY. How many did you get to keep?

ANGELA. Well, that was the tricky part. Because once you have that many rabbits, it's kind of like you either get rid of them all or you become rabbit raisers. And we weren't really set up for that. So we gave one to a lady who worked with my mom, but the others were harder to find homes for. It started to become this stress between my parents, like, "What are we going to do with all these rabbits?" And of course I felt responsible, so...

RANDY. Uh-oh.

ANGELA. A couple of kids from the neighborhood said they wanted one, and I was like great, let's show them all off, so everyone can decide which one they like best. So I bring them out to the front lawn, a few at a time, and I have the other kids watch the ones I drop off, until they're all out there. And at first it's kind of a dream. I mean, my little neighborhood pals and all these adorable bunnies, everyone rolling around on the grass in front of my house? Like the only way it could've been better is if we all had ice cream and the rabbits could talk.

DONALD. *(Sincere, lost in the fantasy.)* What do you think they would say?

PAUL. *(Aside.)* Shh.

ANGELA. Then one of the bunnies takes off.

ESTELLE. No.

ANGELA. It shoots across the lawn and into the bushes. And I'm like, shit. Then another one takes off in a different direction. And one goes under the house, and one runs into the street, and we trap that one behind a parked car, but by the time I get it back to the grass, they've all run off. We would chase down one and think we had it under control, and then another would squirt free and... I just didn't know how fast they were. I'd never seen them run before.

(A moment; considers.)

Why did you want me to tell that story?

PAUL. It reminds me of being in love.

ANGELA. Seriously, Paul?

PAUL. Yes. And I think that's a good thing to be reminded of in a time of mourning. Don, I'm sorry if that makes you uncomfortable.

DONALD. Oh, you know...

ANGELA. Why are you apologizing to him?

PAUL. Estelle and Randy, I'm sorry if that makes you uncomfortable.

ESTELLE. No.

RANDY. Actually –

ANGELA. You really are a piece of work, Paul, you know that?

DONALD. Okay, okay –

PAUL. And that reminds me of being ridiculed by my chronically disappointed ex-girlfriend.

ANGELA. What am I doing here?

PAUL. Which is not something I think is good to be reminded of in a time of mourning.

ESTELLE. Did you catch all the bunnies? Angela?

ANGELA. *(A hard look at **PAUL**; then.)* What?

ESTELLE. Did you catch all the bunnies?

ANGELA. We lost...two.

RANDY. Damn it.

DONALD. They probably just ran off to live somewhere nice.

ESTELLE. How did Cinnamon take it?

PAUL. Unfortunately, they had to give Cinnamon away.

ESTELLE. Really?

ANGELA. After the babies were gone, her personality changed.

ESTELLE. Like, how?

ANGELA. She started to growl a lot.

RANDY. Rabbits don't growl.

PAUL. Really, Randy? Have you known many rabbits?

RANDY. A few.

PAUL. Yeah, when?

RANDY. Hey, you know what, Paul? Just because you're depressed, doesn't mean you have license –

PAUL. I'm not depressed –

RANDY. – To shit on everyone else.

PAUL. I'm not depressed. I'm in mourning, Randy, there's a difference.

RANDY. We're here trying to support you.

PAUL. Did I ask you to come?

DONALD. Hey now –

RANDY. You think I don't have other places to be?

PAUL. No, actually, I don't. And if I'm wrong about that, why don't you go to those places, because truth be told, I'd rather be drinking with Henry the Pedophile right now than with you. At least he *knows* he's a creep.

> (**RANDY** *lunges at* **PAUL** *and* **DONALD** *has to separate them.*)

RANDY. You're a fucking asshole!

DONALD. Stop it!

PAUL. I'm cool, I'm cool.

RANDY. Idiot!

DONALD. Randy!

PAUL. That's all right, Don, he can't help it.

RANDY. What did you say?

PAUL. I think I called you a fucking fuckface.

(*Again* **RANDY** *goes after* **PAUL**, *and again*
DONALD *has to separate them.*)

DONALD. Paul!

ANGELA. God, Paul, you really are an asshole.

DONALD. No! Nobody's an asshole and nobody's a fuckface!
We're all friends! And we're having a nice time!

ESTELLE. What does a rabbit growl sound like?

PAUL. (*If nobody else will.*) I'll show her.

(**ANGELA** *bolts toward* **ESTELLE**, *cutting off*
PAUL, *to make sure she's the one doing the*
instructing. Quietly but audibly, **ANGELA**
growls like a rabbit.)

ESTELLE. No kidding.

ANGELA. Yeah. See, usually a rabbit goes:

(**ANGELA** *pushes air back and forth quickly*
through her teeth.)

ESTELLE. Like a whisper.

ANGELA. Sort of.

(**ANGELA** *does the rabbit whisper again.*
ESTELLE *tries it.*)

(**RANDY** *goes to them and all three try the*
rabbit whisper.)

RANDY. Like this?

ANGELA. Okay, you have to push the air in and out between
your teeth. And don't keep inhaling, it all should
happen using the same bunch of air.

DONALD. With your tongue darting back and forth.

(**DONALD** *joins in, a master of the rabbit*
whisper.)

ANGELA. Yeah, see his lips?

ESTELLE. (*Getting it.*) I got it.

ANGELA. Nice.

RANDY. (*Almost getting it.*) Like this?

ANGELA. *(Shaping her lips to feature buck teeth.)* It helps if you make a rabbit mouth.

DONALD. Watch.

ANGELA. *(To* **DONALD.***)* God, you're so good at it now.

> (**DONALD** *and* **ANGELA** *are now side by side, unconsciously touching as they illustrate the rabbit whisper to* **RANDY,** *who's almost figured out how to do it.)*

> (**PAUL** *watches* **DONALD** *and* **ANGELA,** *wounded by their affection for each other, as he drifts toward the lockers.)*

Okay good, but then if the rabbit's mood changes, it goes:

> (**ANGELA** *growls.)*

> (**RANDY, DONALD,** *and* **ESTELLE** *follow her lead, growling in unison.)*

So if you put it all together, if you're snuggling and they start off making the regular rabbit sound, but then they turn on you, it goes:

> (**ANGELA** *makes the regular rabbit sound and transitions suddenly into a growl.)*

RANDY & ESTELLE. Oooh...

> (**RANDY, DONALD, ESTELLE,** *and* **ANGELA** *do the whisper-to-growl transition.)*

ANGELA. Nice!

PAUL. And that's what Cinnamon started doing all the time. Until she stopped making the regular rabbit sound and was only growling. Soon she was biting off shirt buttons, and then she started biting Angela, right? Her parents had no choice but to demand that the rabbit be gotten rid of. Angela wanted to argue, but the truth is, she was tired of Cinnamon blaming her for everything. She knew the rabbit was right, and the rabbit did too, but unless Cinnamon was willing to forgive her – and clearly she wasn't – the two of them couldn't go on together. See, that's the trouble with being right. It turns you into the angry one. And nobody likes a self-righteous rabbit.

ANGELA. Why do you hate me?

> (**PAUL** *goes to his locker.*)

PAUL. I don't hate you. This is just my heart after it's been put through the meat grinder of life.

> (**PAUL** *opens his locker and pulls out his backpack. He notices something different about it. He looks inside.*)

There is a cat in this bag.

ANGELA. What?

PAUL. There's a cat in this bag.

ESTELLE. What kind of cat?

ANGELA. Let me see.

PAUL. (*Pulling the bag away.*) Who put this cat in this bag?

ANGELA. (*To* **DONALD.**) Are you kidding me?

DONALD. What?

PAUL. Don? Did you put this cat in this bag?

DONALD. Maybe.

> (**PAUL** *looks at the cat again.*)

ANGELA. (*To* **DONALD.**) How could you?

RANDY. Is it alive?

PAUL. Why, in the name of Jesus Christ almighty, is there a cat in this bag?

DONALD. Because they didn't want him at the shelter?

PAUL. Is that supposed to be funny?

DONALD. Dude, it's a present.

PAUL. For me?

DONALD. Yeah.

> (*The cat meows.*)

ANGELA. Let me see it.

PAUL. Back off.

ANGELA. You're scaring it.

PAUL. I will throw this cat down the elevator shaft if any one of you so much as lifts a hand toward me. Okay? I will throw it out the fucking window.

(*To* **ANGELA.**) Was this your idea? Because that would be an extra layer of fucked-up-edness.

ANGELA. You better not let anything happen to that animal.

PAUL. Or what?

ANGELA. Or I will beat your ass in front of all these people.

DONALD. It was my idea, man. She didn't have anything to do with it.

ANGELA. I wouldn't even be here tonight if he didn't manipulate me into coming.

DONALD. You knew we were throwing a party for Paul.

ANGELA. I didn't know you were bringing a cat.

DONALD. I wanted it to be a surprise.

ANGELA. That isn't a surprise, Don. If two people decide against doing something, then one of them goes behind the other's back and does it anyway, that isn't a surprise.

PAUL. So you did know about it.

ANGELA. I knew it was a dumb idea and I wanted no part of it.

DONALD. But baby, just because you think it's a dumb idea –

ANGELA. Don, we decided.

DONALD. No, you decided, and then I made a different decision. Not to spite you, but because I thought it was the right thing to do. Angela, it's not like it's a pound of cocaine. It's a cat.

ANGELA. I am so stupid.

DONALD. Look at it, it's joy and hope –

ANGELA. I came here tonight for you, Don, because it meant something to you.

PAUL. You didn't even want to be here?

ANGELA. I dropped a card off for you, Paul. Did you get my card?

PAUL. Yes.

ANGELA. Okay, and where's my thanks for that?

PAUL. Thank you.

ANGELA. It's not that I don't care about you, Paul. You know that, but I also know how you are –

PAUL. Of course, that's why you broke up with me –

ANGELA. – When you're upset, is what I was going to say. I know how you are when you are upset. Jesus, you make it so hard.

PAUL. To love me?

ANGELA. To talk to you! Just talking to you can be so difficult. Look, you need space. I get it. And I tried explaining that to him.

(To **DONALD**.*)* I thought we understood each other.

DONALD. We do understand each other.

ANGELA. No we don't. We don't understand. I don't understand.

DONALD. Babe –

PAUL. What made you think I would want a new cat? Did I tell you I want a new cat?

DONALD. Not specifically.

PAUL. Because that would be a good reason to get someone a new cat, like if they said they wanted one. Don, do you have any idea what a relief it is to come home from work and – for the first time in seventeen years – not have to clean up someone else's shit?

DONALD. No.

PAUL. Do you have any idea how great a feeling it is to leave something small and precious on the counter, and not have to worry that it'll be knocked down the drain or into some impossibly tiny crevice? Do you know how nice it is to wake up in the morning without cat hair in your beard or underwear? Any idea how restful it is to sleep eight hours without some little paw socking you in the eye? Are your forearms and back covered in scratches? Mine aren't. And it feels terrific. How about discovering, Don, that you can stay out all night and not worry about getting home by a certain time? Or knowing you can visit a foreign country or go to law school, or try online dating? Can you imagine, Don, what it would feel like to deny yourself life's great experiences for nigh on two decades because you were consumed with caring for another living creature, only to wake up one day to realize that you no longer have to deny yourself? Do you know how great a responsibility it is to love a cat? Here. Take it.

> (**PAUL** *offers the bag to* **DONALD.** *After a moment* **DONALD** *reaches for the bag, but* **PAUL** *pulls it back.*)

I am not that bad a man. My sins are not so unforgivable that I deserve to be laden with so great a burden so soon after serving their kind for so long. It's someone else's turn.

> (**PAUL** *offers the bag, then reneges.*)

You ever cut a cat's nails, Don?

DONALD. No.

PAUL. No? So you wouldn't know what a treat it is to not have to cut a cat's nails. Not having to chase it around the apartment and wrap it up in a towel and excise one writhing limb after the next as it screams bloody murder, like you're persecuting its whole family. Do you know how much cat food costs? And litter? And cat toys and cat treats, and trips to the vet? Do you have any idea what it's like to get quoted some exorbitant price for some bullshit cancer treatment for your old-as-dirt cat and just be like, yeah man, that's not something I can pull off right now. You ever mix up your money and your morality like that? Is this thing supposed to be a replacement?! Do you think that's how it works?! Are you a replacement for me? I'm asking: Are you my replacement?

DONALD. I don't think so.

PAUL. And yet you would ask this helpless creature to replace one of the top five cats in history?

DONALD. I didn't know Jennifer was sick. You never said –

PAUL. You intervened in my life. You made a decision to change the course of my affairs because it made you feel good.

DONALD. I think of you as being a person with a lot to give, Paul.

PAUL. I don't want to give anything.

DONALD. You don't mean that.

ANGELA. It's not your job to tell him what he means.

ESTELLE. Can I have the cat?

DONALD. I'm fighting for something here, Angela. Which is more than I can say for you right now.

ANGELA. What are you fighting for?

DONALD. Paul's happiness.

PAUL. I don't want to be happy.

ANGELA. Did you hear that? Did you hear him saying those words? Those words, Don, those are the words he means.

PAUL. I want to be sad and broken.

ANGELA. And that is a shame, Paul, but if that is what you want –

DONALD. No! We have an obligation to pull together as a family to beat back Paul's despair.

PAUL. What do you have against my despair?

DONALD. Paul, I know you think this Cloud of Shitty is you, but it's not. The real you is a gigantic, tender soul, crying out from within, as the Cloud of Shitty tries to strangle it. And maybe I thought this cat would help you realize that, and give you something to fight for, and help you – the real you – to break free.

PAUL. Yet instead of beating back my despair, Don, you have retooled it and made it stronger by injecting it with rage. Because now I hate your fucking guts. And now you have a cat.

ESTELLE. I want the cat. Okay? Paul, if you're not going to take the cat, I would like to have the cat.

PAUL. Is that right? You want to give your life to this cat, Estelle?

ESTELLE. Yes, I do. I'm ready, okay? I've never had a pet before, and I am ready to know what it's like, to experience true companionship. And lord knows it isn't gonna come from anywhere else.

    (A long silence.)

RANDY. I'm sorry?

PAUL. What did you just say?

DONALD. I think she said...

ESTELLE. I want the cat.

RANDY. Did she just say –

ESTELLE. Oh, shut up, Randy, I'm tired of you and all your excuses.

    (Slowly, they encircle **ESTELLE.***)*

PAUL. You've never had a pet?

ESTELLE. No, Paul, I haven't.

DONALD. Because why?

ESTELLE. I don't know, my parents wouldn't let me.

PAUL. Well, I mean, I might buy that from a kid, Estelle, but you're a grown woman.

ESTELLE. Yes, I know that, Paul.

RANDY. Is she allergic?

DONALD. I don't know.

RANDY. Ask her if she's allergic.

PAUL. Are you allergic?

ESTELLE. No, I am not allergic.

DONALD. Are you frightened of them?

ESTELLE. No, not really.

ANGELA. *(Referring not to pets, but to* **ESTELLE** *and* **RANDY.***)* Have you ever tried?

ESTELLE. *(To* **ANGELA.***)* Yes I have.

RANDY. What is she saying?

DONALD. I think she's saying –

PAUL. You never lived with a pet at any time in your life?

ESTELLE. No.

RANDY. *(To* **DONALD.***)* What about a fish? Ask her about fish.

PAUL. A fish?

ESTELLE. No, I never had a fish.

PAUL. A lizard?

ESTELLE. No.

DONALD. Bird?

ESTELLE. Damn it, what's wrong with you people?!

RANDY. What's wrong with us? What kind of a person would go their whole lives without loving an animal?

ESTELLE. I didn't know I was supposed to.

PAUL, DONALD & RANDY. Supposed to? Supposed to?!

ESTELLE. We weren't a family who had animals!

PAUL. What did you have?

ESTELLE. People! We had people! The house was full, and everybody in it was a person!

ANGELA. *(Sympathetic.)* Oh, baby girl.

RANDY. How come you never mentioned this before?

ESTELLE. You never asked.

RANDY.	**ESTELLE.**
Do you have any idea how humiliating this is? To find this out in public?	Not once in all the shifts we worked together. Even when I made it obvious that I wanted to be asked –

DONALD. I'll take the cat.

ESTELLE. *(To* **PAUL***, going for it.)* I said I want the cat.

PAUL. Listen, Estelle, it's a nice gesture, but I can't let that happen.

ESTELLE. Just because I've never had a pet before doesn't mean I wouldn't be good at it now.

PAUL. Sure, in theory.

DONALD. It's my responsibility and I will take the cat.

PAUL. No, you have a God Complex, Don. Before we know it, the cat will be having a bad day and you'll be trying to convince it it had a good one. I will hold on to the cat.

ESTELLE. But I want it.

PAUL. I will find it a proper home, with an owner who is capable of caring for it, one who has not been withholding affection from all God's creatures her entire life and in so doing missed out on the most mystical part of the human drama.

ESTELLE. Which is what?! Somebody tell me, what is it that's so amazing that I've missed out on my entire life?

RANDY. Precisely.

> (**ESTELLE** *goes to* **RANDY** *and kisses him hard. Silence.*)

ESTELLE. (*After a moment, to* **PAUL**.) Why don't you know how to knit, huh? Do you know what you're missing?

> (**ESTELLE** *exits. It's quiet.*)

RANDY. I should probably see if she needs a ride.

> (**RANDY** *calmly goes to the door, combing his hair as he exits.*)

PAUL. Don, I'm going to let you lock up for the weekend changeover.

DONALD. I'm not working.

PAUL. You are now.

DONALD. But I've never done that before, I don't even know the procedures.

PAUL. You'll figure it out.

> (**PAUL** *leaves, taking the kitty bag.* **ANGELA** *won't look at* **DONALD**.)

DONALD. Gosh. That was pretty crazy.

> (*After a moment.*)

You want to hang out for a little bit, help me lock up?

(After a moment.)

Angela?

(After a moment.)

Come in, Angela.

Scene Five

(No one is on shift. It's 3:37 a.m. on Saturday.)

(From elsewhere in the building, many floors below, a faint noise is heard, and the single TV monitor showing the lobby goes black.)

(A louder banging is heard from afar.)

Scene Six

(**ESTELLE** *and* **RANDY** *are in the guards'
post.* **ESTELLE***'s knitting is out, but she isn't
knitting.* **RANDY***, who has just arrived, holds
a deli bag, to-go coffee, and a newspaper.*)

(*It's 8:07 a.m. on Monday.*)

ESTELLE. So, first they knock out the camera in the lobby.

RANDY. No.

ESTELLE. Yes.

RANDY. How many perps?

ESTELLE. Nobody knows.

RANDY. What?!

ESTELLE. You take out the picture, there's no way to tell.
And there weren't any prints, so they must have worn
gloves. Alice says they came in on Spruce Street,
through the side door by the loading dock –

RANDY. Wait, is this HR Alice or front office Alice?

ESTELLE. Front office Alice –

RANDY. Oh my God –

ESTELLE. And she got it all from the cops.

RANDY. Right. So, they knock out the camera...

ESTELLE. Yeah, then they bash in the trash can and the
planter and they murder that big framed poster of the
lighthouse?

RANDY. Jesus Christ. What'd they use?

ESTELLE. I don't know, maybe a baseball bat?

RANDY. All right, then what?

ESTELLE. Then they take off.

RANDY. What do you mean? They didn't steal anything?

ESTELLE. No, they just beat the heck out of the lobby and
left.

RANDY. What kind of animals would do such a thing?

ESTELLE. Some angry guys from a baseball team?

RANDY. And where was the weekend crew when all this happened?

ESTELLE. Hadn't shown up yet. Oh, and get this: Paul and Don are both getting suspended.

RANDY. No. Why Don?

ESTELLE. I guess Paul took off early and gave Don the shift, so Don was the last man in the building.

RANDY. Whoa, whoa, whoa: Are you telling me Paul took off early? He can't do that!

ESTELLE. Well, he did. And now they're both getting suspended for the week, though not simultaneously, which is good, because then there would have been like eighty extra hours to pick up in one week. So we still have to pick up forty extra hours a week for two weeks, which is kinda too bad, but not as bad as it could have been.

RANDY. This is an atrocity. I didn't even notice anything different when I walked in the building.

ESTELLE. I know.

RANDY. Did you get to see it at least?

ESTELLE. No, the weekend crew had cleaned it all up. Now the front office is all "so excited" about what a good job they did.

RANDY. And just the lobby? They didn't go anywhere else?

ESTELLE. Not according to the cameras.

RANDY. I'll do a patrol later today, give it a more thorough look-see.

ESTELLE. I think the cops already reviewed all the tapes.

RANDY. The tapes? The tapes?

(*Re: the monitors.*) Look at this. All these cameras, but you take out one and you sabotage the whole system. This isn't a gig for tapes, Estelle.

(**RANDY** *pulls out egg sandwiches from the deli bag, hands one to* **ESTELLE**, *and takes a seat. They eat and work.*)

ESTELLE. (*The sandwich.*) This is good.

RANDY. Yeah?

ESTELLE. Not too greasy.

RANDY. I asked for extra pepper.

ESTELLE. Thank you.

(*They eat. It's quiet.*)

RANDY. So listen. How many cars have you owned?

ESTELLE. Cars? Maybe two? How many cars have you owned?

RANDY. Four.

ESTELLE. Okay.

RANDY. How many jobs have you had?

ESTELLE. Like, "jobs" jobs?

RANDY. Yeah.

ESTELLE. (*Considers.*) More than two. How many jobs have you –

RANDY. I was married.

ESTELLE. Oh. When?

RANDY. Years ago.

ESTELLE. And how was that?

RANDY. All right. You know, not great.

ESTELLE. Did anything bad happen to her?

RANDY. She moved to Cincinnati.

ESTELLE. Do you have any children?

RANDY. No, thank god. I mean, not that I have anything against kids –

ESTELLE. Good, because I would like to have them someday.

RANDY. All right.

(*They eat.*)

I assume they're asking the weekend crew to cover some of the extra shifts?

ESTELLE. I doubt it.

RANDY. I'm gonna get a cold. You'll see. How much do you want to bet I get a cold? Doesn't matter how much sleep I get or how many vitamins I take, as soon as I start pulling extra shifts, I get a cold.

(It's quiet.)

RANDY. What else? Would you like to have?

ESTELLE. I'd like a cat.

RANDY. All right.

ESTELLE. And a dog.

RANDY. Now, I don't know about a dog –

ESTELLE. And a dog.

Scene Seven

(A park bench on a too-sunny day. **DONALD** *is off work but still in uniform.* **ANGELA** *wears civvies, has a backpack with her.)*

(It's 1:12 p.m. on Thursday, five months after the cat-giving.)

ANGELA. I'm way behind everyone else.

DONALD. You'll catch up.

ANGELA. It's just so much information, I'm like, gah.

DONALD. Is it exciting, though, to be sucking up all those new facts? Like, is your brain a better sponge now that you're a –

(Looking for the words.)

– more mature student?

ANGELA. Maybe. Possible. For certain things. For hard science I think a fresher brain might be better, or at least that's what I tell myself when I'm in the middle of losing my shit. You're good at science, right?

DONALD. No.

ANGELA. How come I thought you were good at science?

DONALD. I don't know. I'm good at history.

ANGELA. Nursing school is a lot of science. And math.

DONALD. Now, I was good at math until they added letters.

ANGELA. Which letters?

DONALD. X, Y, A. B. Yeah, when it was just numbers I was like, what's sixteen times seven? 112. What's twenty-three times nine? 207.

ANGELA. Wow.

DONALD. Right? But then the letters came along and took my swag.

ANGELA. I'm pretty good at math.

DONALD. I believe that.

ANGELA. Just wish I could get someone else to do all the science.

DONALD. But you don't have to be awesome at science to be a good nurse.

ANGELA. You'd be a good nurse.

DONALD. Right.

ANGELA. You would.

DONALD. With these shaky hands? You want to see these pulling out some big-ass needle and sticking it into your arm?

ANGELA. There are many different kinds of nurses one could be, if one decided to become a nurse.

DONALD. No, that's true. Are there a lot of guys in your class?

ANGELA. A few.

DONALD. Are they big?

ANGELA. What do you mean?

DONALD. I don't know, big.

ANGELA. Like –

DONALD. Tall or round?

ANGELA. Some?

DONALD. It's good to be big, if you're gonna be a male nurse. Don't you think?

ANGELA. I don't know.

DONALD. Everybody likes a big male nurse.

ANGELA. I think there are lots of really excellent small male nurses.

DONALD. I don't.

ANGELA. What about you? Are you planning to…"stand guard" for the foreseeable future?

DONALD. Yup, that's the plan.

ANGELA. That's cool.

DONALD. Just keep doing my thing and loving life.

ANGELA. Right on.

DONALD. Try to grow, you know? These days I'm all about being my own teacher?

ANGELA. Nice.

DONALD. Yeah, and that job, as slow as it gets, it really does give me time to think. And right now that's like the most important thing in the world to me.

ANGELA. That's kind of super beautiful.

DONALD. You ever miss it? Being over there with us?

ANGELA. Sometimes.

DONALD. I bet you don't miss the hours, though.

ANGELA. No, I don't miss the hours and I don't miss the work, or lack thereof. Although honestly, this would've been a perfect week to be there. I could be doing all my schoolwork *and* making money, instead of being unemployed and just diving into debt.

DONALD. Yeah, but you got to where you needed to be, right? And you're doing what you need to be doing.

ANGELA. Trying.

DONALD. That's it then. I mean, that's everything.

(Quiet, considers.)

It's kind of shocking how great a breakup it was, don't you think? Just like, how right it felt? For the time. In the same way it feels right now, to be sitting here, talking?

ANGELA. *(Not sure what to make of that.)* Yeah.

DONALD. You know what I mean?

ANGELA. I think so, yeah. Thanks for saying that. I guess I wasn't sure that's how you'd feel.

DONALD. Well, that is how I feel. About what, though?

ANGELA. Not being together.

DONALD. Right, no, that's what I thought you were saying. What, you thought I was going to be like super duper mad?

ANGELA. I didn't know. But I'm glad you feel good about it now.

DONALD. Yeah, I mean, I felt good about it pretty soon after.

ANGELA. Good. I mean, not good, sad.

DONALD. Yeah, no, sad.

ANGELA. But also…good –

DONALD. Right.

ANGELA. Healthy.

DONALD. Good.

ANGELA. Good.

DONALD. I know I had good thoughts about you.

ANGELA. And I totally had good thoughts about you. And I was hoping you were okay, you know, and I was wanting to reach out but feeling like maybe I shouldn't? And then, yeah, just thinking about you and not knowing how you were doing and hoping everything was okay.

DONALD. So you felt good about it too?

ANGELA. I mean, at the time? No. But like you said, it felt right, in the big picture. But also hard.

DONALD. *(Divulging.)* I was a wreck.

ANGELA. No.

DONALD. Yeah, for the first couple of weeks there, I was like, obliterated.

ANGELA. I'm sorry.

DONALD. Hey, you know? You were the first person I cared about like that. And I just wanted to get it right. So, that was bad. In addition to just missing you – your smell and your smile; I was like, *where is she?* And then at some point, I don't know what did it, but it was like, I finally heard it.

ANGELA. What?

DONALD. What you had been saying. About me.

ANGELA. What was I saying?

DONALD. About how I'm always talking this talk, but walking that walk.

ANGELA. Did I say that?

DONALD. Well, not exactly.

ANGELA. Yeah, that doesn't sound like me.

DONALD. But that was the idea, that I would say one thing and do something else.

ANGELA. Okay?

DONALD. And how uncool that was. And how, you said I like to say things to get 'em off my chest, but really, in the end, I just want to control the situation and let everybody else deal.

ANGELA. Right?

DONALD. You don't remember?

ANGELA. I mean, I'm not sure –

DONALD. But so yeah, I heard that. Or thought I heard it. And then I also heard that part about you, which I realized didn't have anything to do with me.

ANGELA. And which part was that?

DONALD. Just how you had been in this pattern of dating where you were going from guy to guy to guy –

ANGELA. Right, and?

DONALD. And just how crazy that was making you feel. I mean, I don't know if you used the word crazy –

ANGELA. No.

DONALD. But you did say it felt wrong. Not morally wrong.

ANGELA. No.

DONALD. But emotionally? Didn't you? Something like that? This is what I remember:

ANGELA. Okay?

DONALD. You said you felt like you could hear all the voices of the different guys you had dated, talking to you in your head, telling you what you should do and how you should be, and that you were just like, tired of it. And how you wanted to hear your own voice, without everyone else chiming in.

ANGELA. Go on.

DONALD. And that's when I realized, you know, as long as you're feeling that way about yourself, you're not really available to anyone else, least of all me.

ANGELA. This is what I remember: I remember being at work the week you weren't there, and us not talking –

DONALD. 'Cause you didn't want to –

ANGELA. I know, I know – you were suspended and I needed to think – I'm just saying, I remember that week of not talking. And you not being there. And me feeling like myself. And I remember you coming back, and us talking again, and me feeling less like myself. I remember thinking it wasn't right. And deciding I wanted other things. And I remember turning in my resignation, and I remember us talking up on the roof –

DONALD. Right, and you said –

ANGELA. And I remember being sad for a long, long time, and then I remember getting over it.

DONALD. Ah. Yes. Yes.

Scene Eight

(The security guards' post. **PAUL** *is nearly done with his shift;* **DONALD** *is midway through his.* **DONALD** *is a less hopeful man now.)*

(They listen to hectic, instrumental lounge jazz from the early 80s.[*] The song is intense. They bop along with their heads when they must.)

(It's 3:52 a.m. on Wednesday, eight months after the cat-giving.)

PAUL. There's an implicit fuck you to it.

DONALD. Right. What's it called again?

PAUL. "Nice Try."

*(**PAUL** turns the music back up, then skips to another song,[*] a haunting, melancholy sax-lead instrumental.)*

This one's called "You're Always With Me."

(The two listen for a long time, occasionally consulting the monitors.)

I have to tell you something.

*(**PAUL** turns the music down.)*

I sent her a card.

DONALD. *(Taking that in.)* What'd you say?

PAUL. Congratulations.

DONALD. Well, I bet she'll appreciate that.

PAUL. I know we kinda said we weren't going to send her anything.

---

*A license to produce *Red-Handed Otter* does not include a performance license for any third-party or copyrighted music. Licensees should create an original composition or use music in the public domain. "Nice Try" and "You're Always With Me" are fictional titles. For further information, please see Music Use Note on page 3.

DONALD. Right.

PAUL. I just felt like I had to say something.

DONALD. Okay.

PAUL. You know?

DONALD. If that's what you had to do.

PAUL. *(Considers.)* You didn't send her anything?

DONALD. No.

PAUL. See, that makes me feel like an asshole.

DONALD. It's not like we made a binding pact.

PAUL. I didn't mean it. That's the problem. I mean, there were things I wanted to say that I actually meant, but congratulations wasn't one of them.

DONALD. Yeah, I thought that's why we weren't going to send anything.

PAUL. I think I forgot about the why. It was because I didn't mean it. Not that I don't wish her well. But that's not the same as congratulations.

DONALD. No, it's different.

PAUL. If I really had to say something, it should have been more like, "Live In Relative Peace." Or, "Don't Suffer More Than You Have To." But those aren't good cards.

DONALD. No.

PAUL. So, basically, I misled you and deceived myself.

DONALD. And you sent someone an insincere message for a wedding present.

PAUL. Shitcakes.

> *(Considers.)*

She didn't invite you, did she? To the wedding.

DONALD. Man, I told you she didn't.

PAUL. Yeah, but I was withholding information from you, I thought maybe you were doing the same.

> *(They listen.)*

I like weddings. All the married people talking about the day they got married. The single people getting hammered and looking for someone to make out with.

The little kids trying to strangle each other with their little neckties.

DONALD. The dancing.

PAUL. Oh yeah, the first dance. The train dance. The hora. Those two people saying those things to each other in front of all those other people.

(*They listen.*)

Would you have gone if she invited you?

DONALD. I doubt it.

PAUL. Yeah, that's probably why she didn't invite me.

DONALD. Why?

PAUL. Because she knew you wouldn't go, so then it would've been just me, flirting with all her friends.

Either that or she thought, shit, if I invite Paul, then I have to invite Estelle and Randy too, and all of a sudden you're talking about 500 people.

DONALD. Estelle and Randy are going.

PAUL. Those fucking fuckers. Why them?

DONALD. She likes them. They do stuff together.

PAUL. But instead of us?

DONALD. Yes, dude, she invited the couple she's actually friends with over the guy she was madly in love with – and you.

PAUL. (*Considers a long time.*) You know, Angela and I went out for close to a year.

DONALD. Right?

PAUL. How long did you guys go out for, three months?

DONALD. Four.

PAUL. Oh, okay.

DONALD. Depending on when you start counting.

PAUL. Uh-huh?

DONALD. (*Considers.*) You know she spent most of the time you were together trying to figure out how to break up with you, right?

PAUL. No, I didn't know that.

DONALD. Yeah, yeah, I guess it was pretty much all she could think about.

PAUL. *(Considers.)* Remember when you first started working here?

DONALD. Uh-huh, when you two were still going out?

PAUL. Right.

DONALD. Right?

PAUL. So, one day she asked if I thought you might be a little retarded.

DONALD. Huh.

PAUL. Yeah. Not based on anything you said, but just like, from how you look.

DONALD. And what did you say?

PAUL. I said I didn't think so. Although I told her, because my high school was mainstreamed, so I had a developmentally disabled kid in my biology class, and I said, theoretically, the company could hire someone like that and just not tell us.

DONALD. It must have been hard on you when we first started fucking around.

PAUL. Not really.

DONALD. I mean if my girl started dating some retarded-looking guy, right in front of my face?

PAUL. I'm the one who broke in and trashed the lobby.

DONALD. What?

PAUL. After I left here that night of the party, I went to a diner with the cat, and we sat there for a while. I ordered us tuna melts. And then I drove home and I dropped the cat off and I got my ski mask and gloves and I came back here and I let myself in on Spruce Street, since I knew you wouldn't know to lock up that door, and then I walked down the side stairs, took out that main camera and then I beat the shit out of that lobby. And it felt good.

DONALD. You got me suspended.

PAUL. You stole my girlfriend.

> (**DONALD** *leaps for* **PAUL**'s *throat, tackling him, and they wrestle. The fight is epic, childish, galumphing, and fierce.*)
>
> (**PAUL** *gets the upper hand at first...*)

You done?

> (**DONALD** *soon gains control.*)

DONALD. You ruined everything! Why? Why?!

> (**PAUL** *manages to push* **DONALD** *off. They struggle to catch their breath.*)

PAUL. The cat told me to do it.

> (*Slowly, they get to their feet.*)
>
> (*After a moment,* **DONALD** *and* **PAUL** *settle. They return to their seats. They breathe. They listen to music.*)
>
> (**PAUL** *gets up and collects his things.*)

DONALD. How is the cat?

PAUL. You want to know how the cat is? The cat is destroying my fucking life. Look at this.

> (**PAUL** *comes back to the desk and pulls out his phone to show* **DONALD** *pictures.*)

DONALD. He's filling out.

PAUL. Yeah, he's handsome as shit. But do you see what he's sleeping on?

DONALD. Is that a sculpture?

PAUL. It's my dinner plate.

DONALD. Where's your dinner?

PAUL. Under the cat.

DONALD. He's eating it?

PAUL. No, why would he eat it when he can just walk over there and take a big nap on it? I go to the bathroom for two seconds, come back to the table, my burrito is covered in cat. I'm like, hey, get the fuck off my dinner. He's like, hey, you should be thankful I'm not sleeping on your fucking computer.

DONALD. He's got a lot of nerve.

PAUL. Shameless. This cat doesn't feel guilty about anything. Okay, and then there's this. In the midst of the villainy, he'll pull this.

> (*Shows* **DONALD** *another phone pic.*)

You know what that is?

DONALD. What?

PAUL. Crescent cat. 'Cause he thinks he's some kind of half-moon.

> (*More pics now.*)

But then, what's this?

DONALD. That doesn't look like a cat.

PAUL. It looks like a monkey, doesn't it?

DONALD. Yeah.

PAUL. Do you know why?

DONALD. Why?

PAUL. Because now he's a monkey cat. What about this? What's this?

DONALD. Huh. There he almost looks like a rat.

PAUL. Because that's rat cat. And here, wait...did you ever see a cat who is also a dragon?

DONALD. No.

PAUL. Now you have. What about owl cat?

DONALD. That's a wise expression.

PAUL. And what's this? I mean, what is this?!

DONALD. Now that's a weird cat.

PAUL. That is a rhombus cat. Where does it come from? How does it get that way? Nobody knows. It shouldn't be possible, yet here it is, asking to be fed yet again. What else? Chicken cat. Horse cat.

DONALD. That's a cool vest.

PAUL. Now you know why I call him Cat of a Thousand Cats. Every time you look he's a different cat. And the worst part is, he thinks I'm his toy. I walk into the apartment, he's like, hey, the scratching post is back.

DONALD. And still no luck finding him a home?

PAUL. Nothing. The first few months, I was interviewing people a couple times a week, sending out e-mails, putting up fliers. I must have talked to thirty-five, forty people.

DONALD. Nobody wanted him?

PAUL. Oh, they wanted him, but they're crazy, these people. I mean, half of them look homeless, and of the ones who don't, half of them already have six cats. You know, and then some, they meet the cat and are instantly affectionate with it in a way that you just know is not appropriate. I'm like, come on, man, you don't even know that cat. And the rest, it's just obvious that as soon as the cat reveals its true nature, these people are going to freak the fuck out and want to get rid of it. And is that something I want on my hands?

DONALD. No.

PAUL. There was this one lady, Cathy, single mom, I thought we were golden. Had her come over, introduced her to the cat. They obviously had a nice rapport, but nothing too intimate. I said okay, go home, think about it, I'll think about it, let's see what happens. That night she calls me, says she'd really like to have the cat, you know, her kids want a cat. I say, okay, the cat's yours. Next day I'm in the car, cat's in the carrier next to me, I got the extra food, toys, litter, I mean – full disclosure: I'm not only about to give this lady a cat, I'm also giving her like $150 in cat paraphernalia. But she lives up in the hills, I don't know the area, so I call her to double-check my directions. She picks up the phone and I am sucker-punched, literally clocked in the face, by a tidal wave of volume coming out of this phone. I mean, it sounds like Mardi Gras over there. And I'm like, whoa, Cathy, that's quite a commotion, everything okay? And she's like oh yeah, that's just my fourteen-year-old, he invited some of his skateboard friends over, they're having a "Welcome the Cat" party, as if that's something I'd be familiar with. And I look at the cat next to me, right, and the cat is quaking just from being in the vicinity of this phone that I'm holding next to my ear. And I say to Cathy, I say, "Gosh, Cathy, I'm not sure if that's really the best way to help a cat adjust to a new environment, you know, with like a whole team of fourteen-year-old boys screaming at it." And Cathy says, "Well, I don't think that's anything you have to worry about, Paul." And I say, "Well Cathy, then I don't think this is your cat." And I hang up the phone.

DONALD. Just like that.

PAUL. Just like that. She leaves me these messages, calling me names – "Who do you think you are?!" Blah, blah, blah – threatening to send this army of teenagers over to kick my ass. Man. And I'm telling you, she was one of the good candidates.

(Considers.)

Where in the fuck is Estelle, by the way?

DONALD. You can take off.

PAUL. Naw-naw, it's cool. Plus I want to make her feel bad for taking my spot at the wedding.

DONALD. What are you going to do with it?

PAUL. What?

DONALD. The cat.

PAUL. I don't know. What can I do? Wait until the right person comes along.

DONALD. What if they don't ever come? What if you wait and wait, and the right person never comes along?

PAUL. They will. The right person will come, Don. And when they do it will be undeniable and true.

DONALD. *(Considers.)* She made me feel like a winner.

PAUL. Well, now she's going to make her husband feel that way.

(They consider.)

End of Play